TREASURE ISLAND

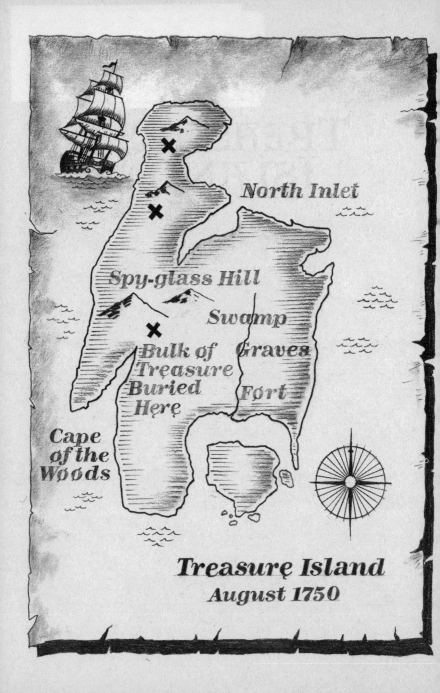

TREASURE ISLAND

by Robert Louis Stevenson
adapted by Lisa Norby
illustrated by Paul Wenzel

A STEPPING STONE BOOK™
Random House 🏠 New York

Text copyright © 1990 by Random House, Inc. Illustrations copyright © 1990
by Paul Wenzel. Cover illustration copyright © 2004 by Corey Wolfe. All rights
reserved under International and Pan-American Copyright Conventions.
Published in the United States by Random House Children's Books, a division
of Random House, Inc., New York, and simultaneously in Canada by Random
House of Canada Limited, Toronto. Originally published in a slightly different
form by Random House, Inc., in 1990.

www.randomhouse.com/kids

Library of Congress Cataloging-in-Publication Data
Norby, Lisa.
Treasure Island / by Robert Louis Stevenson ; adapted by Lisa Norby ;
illustrations by Paul Wenzel.
    p.   cm. — (A Stepping stone book classic)
SUMMARY: An innkeeper's son finds a treasure map that leads him to a
pirate's fortune.
ISBN 0-679-80402-1 (trade) — ISBN 0-679-99429-7 (lib. bdg.)
[1. Buried treasure—Fiction. 2. Pirates—Fiction. 3. Adventure and
adventurers—Fiction.] I. Stevenson, Robert Louis, 1850–1894.
Treasure Island.   II. Wenzel, Paul (Paul Edward), ill.   III. Title.
IV. Series. PZ7.N7752Tr 2001 [Fic]—dc21 00068323

Printed in the United States of America   35 36 37 38 39 40

1. The Old Sea Dog

Squire Trelawney and Dr. Livesey have asked me, Jim Hawkins, to write down the story of Treasure Island. I will tell you everything, just as it happened. The only thing I won't tell you is where the island is. That's because there is still treasure buried there.

To begin my story, I must go back to the time when my father kept the Admiral Benbow Inn. I still remember the day when a strange new guest turned up at our door. He was an old sailor—tall and strong, dressed in a dirty blue coat. His hands were rough. His fingernails were black and broken. A long white scar ran across one cheek. Just looking at it made my knees tremble.

I watched the old sailor as he came up the road to our door. Our inn stood on a high cliff. At the foot of the cliff was the ocean. The stranger stared out at the waves for a long time. Then he started singing to himself. It was the first time I heard the old sea song that I was to hear so often:

"Fifteen men on the dead man's chest. Yo-ho-ho, and a bottle of rum!"

The old sailor's face was always dirty. His clothes were in rags. But he acted like a man who was used to giving orders. We called him the captain.

The best chair in our parlor was right next to the fireplace. The captain claimed that chair right away. Night after night he would sit there staring into the fire. But when other sailors came to the inn he stayed out of sight. He would hide behind the heavy curtain at the parlor door and spy on our new guests.

One day the captain told me that he wanted me to keep an eye out for an old seafaring man with one leg. I had to promise to warn him if the one-legged man showed up. In return, he would give me a silver coin at the beginning of every month.

The thought of that one-legged stranger gave me nightmares. I used to dream about him on stormy nights. In my dreams, he was horrible-looking. He would leap up out of nowhere and chase after me. I really earned that silver coin!

I was not afraid of the captain himself, but a lot of people were. When he started drinking rum, he forgot his quiet ways. He would sing old sea songs in a loud voice and force the other guests at the inn to sing along. And the stories he told! They were all about storms at sea, and pirates, and men being forced to walk the plank.

But the frightening stories did not stop people from coming to the inn to hear them. The captain brought excitement to our quiet English village. Some of the young men even admired him. They called him a "true sea dog" and a "real old salt."

That winter my father fell ill. Dr. Livesey used to come from the village to take care of him. One night, when the doctor was at the inn, the captain was drinking rum. He started to sing his favorite song: "Fifteen men on the dead man's chest . . ."

Dr. Livesey kept on talking, and the captain yelled at him to keep quiet.

The doctor paid no attention. Then the captain pulled a knife.

Dr. Livesey wasn't the least bit afraid. "Put that knife away, or I'll see you hanged," he warned the captain.

The captain glared at Dr. Livesey. But he did as he was told.

Before the doctor left, he had a piece of advice for the captain. "If you don't stop drinking rum, the world will soon be rid of you," he told him.

The captain ignored the warning. "I have worse things to be afraid of than drink," he told me later.

I didn't know what our strange guest was talking about. What was he so afraid of? Was it the man with one leg? It was hard to imagine anyone evil enough to throw a scare into the captain.

2. The Black Spot

Soon after that night, strange things began to happen at our inn.

The first was the arrival of a thin, yellow-skinned man with two fingers missing from his left hand. The man walked in as I was setting the tables for breakfast. "Is my mate Bill here?" he asked.

"I don't know any Bill," I said.

"You probably call him the captain," said the man.

The captain had gone out for a walk. He would be coming back any minute. I wanted to warn him, but the stranger shoved me aside. When the captain came in the front door, he was there waiting.

"Bill," said the man. "You know me, Bill. It's your old shipmate."

The captain gasped. "Black Dog!"

The captain and Black Dog sent me out of the room. Soon they were yelling at each other. I heard a loud crash. Then came the sound of a man screaming in pain. Black Dog came running out of the room, with the captain chasing him. Both men had knives and were slashing away at each other.

Black Dog was cut on the shoulder. He ran out the door and down the path as fast as he could. The captain could hardly stand up.

"Are you hurt?" I cried.

Before he could answer, he fell to the floor. I ran for Dr. Livesey. He said the captain wasn't wounded. He had had a stroke.

The doctor helped me get the captain to his bed. When we unbuttoned his shirt, we saw the name Billy Bones tattooed on one arm. On his chest was another big tattoo of a man hanging from a gallows.

I thought the captain was done for. But the next morning he was wide awake and calling for his rum. "Old Flint's crew is after me," he growled. "Black Dog isn't the worst of them. It's my old sea chest they want. The one where I keep all my things. If I don't get away, they will tip me the black spot."

"What is the black spot?" I asked.

"It's a call, mate," said the captain. "A call."

A call to what? I didn't understand. But I had no time to worry about the captain. That same evening my father died.

I didn't give Captain Billy Bones another thought until the day after my father's funeral. It was a wet, foggy afternoon. The whole world looked gray. I was standing in the doorway, thinking sad thoughts about my father, when at once I saw a blind beggar coming up the road. He wore a long cape with a hood drawn over his face.

"Where am I?" he demanded.

"The Admiral Benbow," said I.

The blind man reached out and grabbed my arm. He squeezed it—

hard. "Take me to the captain," he ordered.

I had never heard a voice so cruel and cold. It scared me more than the pain in my arm. I did what he said.

The captain had started carrying his long knife with him everywhere. It was sitting on the table in front of him as the blind beggar and I came into the parlor. But when he saw us, the captain didn't reach for his knife. He went pale with fright.

The blind man handed the captain a folded piece of paper. "Now that's done," he said. Seconds later he disappeared into the fog. But I could hear his cane go tap-tap-tapping down the path.

The captain unfolded the paper and stared at it. The paper was cut into a circle. One whole side of it was colored black. The captain turned the paper over and read what was on the other side. "Ten o'clock," he said. "I have six hours."

Now I understood what the black spot meant. It meant death. In a few hours the captain's enemies were coming back to kill him.

But the captain didn't have even that long. Suddenly he grabbed his throat. Then he fell face down on the floor. His fear of the black spot had brought on another stroke. And this time, the captain was dead.

I burst into tears. I had never liked the captain. But he was the second dead man I had seen in a few days. I wasn't crying for the captain—I was crying for my poor father. And for myself.

3. The Sea Chest

As soon as I could wipe the tears from my eyes, I ran and told my mother the whole story. We didn't know what we should do. The captain owed us money. He probably had gold in his sea chest. But what about the captain's enemies? They were coming back in a few hours. I was sure they planned to take the captain's money. If we took it first, they might kill us.

My mother was no coward. "We need that money and I mean to have it," she said. "The key to the captain's sea chest must be on his body."

My heart was beating fast. But of course I couldn't run away and leave my mother alone. We hurried to the parlor. Quickly I searched through the captain's pockets. There was no key! Finally I found it hanging on a string around his neck.

We took the key and went up to the captain's room. My mother opened the chest. It was stuffed full of the captain's things. At the very bottom was a packet of papers—and a cloth bag full of gold coins.

Just then I heard a tap-tap-tapping. The sound brought my heart into my mouth. It was the blind man's cane, tapping on the frozen road.

"Take it all and let's get out of here!" I cried.

But my mother was an honest woman. She only wanted what she was owed. She started to count out the money, coin by coin. She counted very slowly. Before she could finish, we heard a low whistle. The blind beggar's friends were close by!

We had to get away—fast. My mother took the money she had already counted. I reached into the chest and grabbed the packet of papers. If we weren't going to get all Billy Bones's gold, we might as well have his papers. Maybe they would turn out to be worth something.

We ran outside and hurried down the path to the village. I could hear footsteps behind us. When I turned around, I saw a lantern winking in the twilight.

Luckily, we were near the stream that ran between our inn and the village. I helped my mother scramble down the steep stream bank. She hid under the bridge. But I was curious. I crept back to see what was going on.

There were seven or eight men in all, and the blind beggar was their leader. He stayed outside in the road. The others rushed into the inn. They found the captain's body. Then they charged upstairs to look for his sea chest.

Suddenly one of the men leaned out the window of the captain's room. "They've been here before us," he shouted. "Do you hear that, Pew? The chest is opened."

Pew must have been the blind man's name. "Is it there?" he called back.

"The money is."

Pew swore. He wasn't interested in the money. "It's Flint's papers I want," he said.

"We don't see them here," the man in the window answered.

"It's the people from the inn. It's that boy!" Pew shouted. "I wish I had put his eyes out!"

The men began to search the inn. I could hear them kicking in doors and turning over the furniture.

Then I heard horses galloping up the road from the village. Blind Pew's helpers ran in all directions. Not one of them stopped to help him. "Johnny! Black Dog! Dirk!" he called out. "You won't leave me!"

But the others were already gone. Just then the horsemen came over the hill. Blind Pew started to run. He was so confused that he ran right into the path of the horses. The horsemen tried to stop, but it was too late. Down went Pew. His cry of terror rang out into the night. Then he cried out no more. He was dead, stone dead.

The men on horseback offered to take me to Dr. Livesey so we could tell him what had happened. We finally found the doctor at the house of Squire Trelawney, the richest man in the area.

The squire's house was large and fine. A servant led us to the library, where the walls were lined from floor to ceiling with books. The glow from the fireplace lit up the room.

The squire and the doctor listened to my story. When Dr. Livesey heard that my mother and I had been brave enough to search for the gold, he slapped his leg. "Bravo!" he said.

Squire Trelawney got very excited when I told him that the blind man had talked about someone named Flint. "Flint was the bloodthirstiest pirate that ever sailed!" he cried.

Dr. Livesey was excited too. "I wonder if those papers show where Flint buried his treasure," he said.

Dr. Livesey took a pair of scissors from his doctor's bag and began to cut open the sealed packet. The squire and I looked over his shoulder.

Inside was a sort of diary. On one page there were a lot of numbers. It seemed to be a record of the money the pirates had stolen. On another page was a set of directions. They told how to find the island where the treasure was buried.

Besides the book, there was a folded sheet of paper. Its edges were sealed shut with wax. Carefully, the doctor slit open the seals. Out fell a map of the island!

The map showed that the island was about nine miles long. One of the big hills in the center of the island was marked "Spy-glass Hill." There were other names, too. And three X's made with red ink. Next to the third red X, someone had written in small, neat letters: "bulk of treasure buried here."

That was all. But the squire and the doctor were delighted.

"This is what Pew's men were after," said the squire. "But you, Jim, were too quick for them. Now Flint's gold

is ours for the taking! I'll start for Bristol tomorrow. In three weeks I will have the best ship in England."

The squire outlined his plan: We were going on a treasure hunt. He would hire the ship and pay for the voyage. Dr. Livesey would be the ship's doctor, and I, Jim Hawkins, would go along as the cabin boy. We were all going to be rich. "We'll have money to eat," the squire promised.

"Count me in," said Dr. Livesey. "But there is one man I'm afraid of."

"Who?" asked the squire.

"You," said Livesey. "You talk too much. We are not the only men who know about this paper."

But the squire promised he would keep our secret. The very next day he left for Bristol to find a ship for our adventure.

4. I Go to Bristol

Finding a ship took longer than the squire thought it would. While he was in Bristol I spent long hours studying the treasure map. I wondered what we would find when we got to the island. Strange animals? Wild savages? In all my dreams, I never imagined anything as strange and terrible as what lay in store for us.

Finally the squire's letter arrived. It was addressed to the doctor.

Dear Livesey,
The ship is bought. She lies at anchor, ready for sea. She is a sweet ship. A child could sail her. Her name is the *Hispaniola*.

The squire had other news, too. He had hired a captain named Smollett. And he had hired a cook for the voyage. The cook's name was Long John Silver. Long John had only one leg, but that was proof that he was a hero. He had been in the navy, and he had lost a leg fighting for his country.

Long John owned a tavern called the Spy-glass Inn. But now he wanted to go to sea again. The squire wrote that Long John had been a big help to him. He knew all the sailors in town. He had helped the squire pick the ones we were taking along on our adventure.

Two days later I went down to Bristol. The squire's servant Tom Redruth went with me. He was coming along on the voyage too. And so were two other of the squire's men— Mr. Hunter and Mr. Joyce.

The squire met us when we arrived. He was wearing a blue sea officer's uniform. He had even started walking like a sailor! He was having a wonderful time. Clearly he was very happy to see us.

"When do we sail?" I cried.

"Sail!" said he. "We sail tomorrow!"

After I had something to eat, the squire gave me a note to deliver. It was addressed to John Silver at the Spy-glass Inn.

Ever since I read the squire's letter, I had been worried about this John Silver. Was he the one-legged sailor of my nightmares?

When I saw Long John, I felt ashamed of myself for being afraid. True, Long John Silver had only one leg. But he looked nothing like the monster of my imagination.

Long John had a plain, honest face. He was a hard worker, too. He used his crutch to hop around the tavern, as lively as a bird.

And how that man could talk! "Hawkins, my lad," he said to me, "you are smart as paint. I can see that right away. You and I should get on well." That day he told me many stories about life at sea. Soon I had told him my story, too—all about Blind

Pew and what had happened at the Admiral Benbow Inn. Long John acted shocked.

Long John treated me like a grownup. He made me feel important. Ever since my father died I had been lonely. I wanted so much to believe that Long John was really my friend!

Dr. Livesey arrived in Bristol later in the afternoon. That night we all slept on the *Hispaniola*. In the morning, just after sunrise, all the sailors took their places on deck. The anchor came up. The ship's sails caught the wind. Soon we were racing out of the harbor.

Long John Silver was up on deck too. "So, ho, mates!" he cried. "We're off."

"Let's have a song," one of the men called out to him.

Long John started to sing: "Fifteen men on the dead man's chest . . ."

In one voice all the men answered back: "Yo-ho-ho, and a bottle of rum!"

That was Billy Bones's song! It seemed strange that Long John and the crew all knew it too. Well, I thought, maybe all sailors sing that song. Anyway, it was too late to worry about that now. We were already on our way to Treasure Island.

5. The Voyage

From the beginning of the voyage Captain Smollett was unhappy. "The men know more about this cruise than I do," he told the squire. "I don't call that fair. They know we are going in search of treasure. They say you have a map with three red X's on it."

"I never told that!" the squire cried. "Not to a soul!"

I knew the squire talked too much. But I believed him when he said he never told anyone about the map. I hadn't told Long John, either. How the men knew was a mystery.

Then one night the first mate disappeared.

"He must have fallen overboard," said Captain Smollett. "It could have been hours ago." It was too late to go back to look for him.

After the first mate disappeared, Long John seemed to take over. All the men looked up to him.

Long John kept the ship running smoothly. Even rough seas didn't stop him from getting around. He strung ropes across the deck. When the *Hispaniola* rolled and tossed, he would hang on to the ropes and pull himself along. He never asked for help.

"He's no common man," one sailor told me. "He can talk like a book. And brave! A lion's nothing alongside of him! In his younger days he could take on four men at a time."

I spent many hours down in the ship's kitchen, which the sailors called the galley. While Long John cooked, I kept him company. He told me lots of stories about his travels.

Long John introduced me to his pet parrot, too. "Hawkins," he said, "this here is Cap'n Flint. This bird may be two hundred years old."

"Pieces of eight! Pieces of eight!" the bird screamed. "Pieces of eight!"

Long John explained that pieces of eight were a kind of gold coin. The parrot had learned those words somewhere in her travels. "Cap'n Flint has been all over the world," he said. "She's seen some evil deeds. That's why I named her after the famous pirate."

The rest of the voyage passed quickly. The crew seemed happy. Squire Trelawney was a kind master. He was always giving out extra treats. He even kept a barrel of apples on deck so that the men could have one anytime they wanted.

Soon we were only a day or so away from Treasure Island. Before I went to bed that night, I decided to help myself to an apple. The barrel was almost empty by now, so I had to climb all the way inside it to get the fruit. It was dark inside the barrel. And quiet, too. I decided to sit there and rest for a while. The ship was rocking from side to side. Soon I started to feel sleepy. I closed my eyes.

I woke up to the sound of voices. Long John had come up on deck. With him was Dick, the youngest sailor in the crew.

Long John was telling Dick a story. "I sailed with Cap'n England, then with Flint," I heard him saying. "It was with Flint that I lost my leg. Old Pew

lost his deadlights—his eyes—at the same time."

I was about to jump out of the barrel when I heard Long John mention Pew. The name made me tremble with fear. Now I knew the truth. Long John had never been in the navy. He was a pirate! One of Flint's old crew!

"Where are Flint's men now, you ask?" Long John went on. "Well, old Pew is dead. But most of them are on board here."

"Ah," said the young sailor. "He was the best of them all. Old Flint."

"You are smart as paint, young fellow," said Long John. "So I'll talk to you like a man. I mean to come back from this voyage a gentleman of fortune."

Long John was making friends with Dick the same way that he had made friends with me. My feelings were hurt. I was jealous. Then I remembered that I had worse things to worry about. Long John was the very man Captain Bones had been so afraid of. He had helped the squire pick the crew. And most of the men he picked were pirates, just like him. Now he was planning a mutiny. The pirates were going to take over the ship and steal the treasure.

Soon another sailor came along—a man named Israel Hands.

"Dick's with us," said Long John.

"I know Dick is with us," said Israel Hands. "The question is, when are we going to make our move?"

"At the last possible minute," said Long John. "The squire and the doctor have the treasure map. I don't know where it is, do I? We'll let them find the stuff and help us get it on board. Then I'll finish them off." He laughed. "I'll wring Trelawney's neck myself."

I was terrified. Long John was going to kill us all!

Just then Long John said he was thirsty. "Jump up, lad, and get me an apple," he told Dick.

Dick got up and came near the barrel. I was too scared to move.

Israel Hands saved my life. "Forget about apples," he said. "Let's have a drink of rum."

Long John gave Dick the key to the storeroom. But he and Israel Hands stayed right where they were. I was starting to wonder how I would ever get out of the barrel without being seen. But then the lookout gave a shout: "Land ho!"

Everyone rushed to the rail. No one saw me scramble out of the barrel. The whole crew was staring at three hills on the horizon. By the light of the moon you could just see them. We

had found our island. Treasure Island!

Captain Smollett took out a map and looked for a good place to land. Long John hurried to look over the captain's shoulder. But the captain's map was a copy. It wasn't the one that showed where the treasure was. Long John frowned. He must have been awfully disappointed.

When no one else was listening, I asked the squire, Dr. Livesey, and Captain Smollett to meet me in the cabin. As soon as we were alone, I told them what I had heard.

"What a fool I was!" cried the squire.

"We can't turn back now," said Captain Smollett. "The crew will not obey me. We will have to bide our time. Silver doesn't know we are onto him. Surprise is on our side.

"And you, Jim," the captain added, "will be our eyes and ears."

Counting Hunter, Joyce, and Redruth, there were seven of us in all. There were nineteen sailors in the crew, including Long John. I couldn't see how biding our time would do any good. I was sure we would never leave the island alive.

6. My Shore Adventure

When the sun came up, I had my first good look at Treasure Island. The trees were a strange shade of green. They made me think of poison. There was no breeze at all. The air had a nasty smell, like rotting leaves. In the distance, the hills rose up. The tops of the hills were naked gray rock. Nothing seemed to grow there but a few flat-topped pine trees.

This was the island of my dreams.

The place where I had hoped to get rich. But now I hated the very sight of it.

The crew was in an evil mood too. It was easy to guess why. Now that we had found the island, they were getting greedy. They wanted to kill us right away.

Captain Smollett came up with a plan. He would give the crew a day off. They could take the lifeboats and go ashore. Long John Silver would go along as their leader. Maybe the whole crew would go. Then we could lift anchor and sail away.

But Long John was too smart to take all the sailors with him. He left Israel Hands and five others on the ship.

Even so, we were glad to see Long John go ashore. We knew he would try to talk sense to the men. He would tell them to be patient. At least that would give us more time.

At the last minute I decided to hide under a folded sail in one of the lifeboats. Maybe I could spy on Long John and find out his plans.

As soon as we got to the beach I ran into the woods. But after a while I sneaked back to where the sailors were. Long John didn't see me coming. From my hiding place in the trees, I could hear him talking to a sailor named Tom.

"This is your last chance," Long John told Tom. "Join us, or else."

Just then I heard a long, drawn-out scream. The sound was so terrible that even the birds were frightened. They rose up into the air and circled overhead.

Tom jumped. "What was that?" he asked Long John.

But Long John just smiled. "That'll be Alan," he said.

Suddenly I realized that we had been wrong. All the sailors had not been on Long John's side after all. Alan had been loyal to us. And now the pirates had killed him.

Tom had figured this out too. "Alan!" he cried. "But I will do my duty. Kill me, too, if you can. I defy you."

With that, brave Tom started to walk away. But he did not get far. Long John picked up his crutch and threw it after him. The crutch hit Tom in the back. He threw up his hands and went down. Moving like lightning, Long John hopped to where Tom was lying. He pulled out a knife and buried it deep in Tom's back.

Suddenly the whole world swam away from me. Everything was topsy-turvy. I felt dizzy. But I knew I had

to save myself. If Long John knew I was hiding nearby, he would stab me, too.

I ran away as fast as I could. Soon I came to one of the twin hills near the center of the island.

All of a sudden I realized that someone, or something, was following me. The figure ran from tree to tree. Every so often I caught a glimpse of it. It hardly looked human. It was so bent over that when it ran, its arms almost dragged along the ground. I thought about stories I had heard of wild men. And cannibals. I was even more scared of this creature than I had been of Long John Silver.

But I could not run fast enough to get away. Finally I gave up. "Who are you?" I asked in a loud voice.

"Ben Gunn," the thing answered. "I am poor Ben Gunn."

The creature stepped out from behind a tree. I saw that it was a man after all. A very strange-looking man. He was dressed in rags. His hair was long and tangled. His skin was so sunburned it was almost black. Even his lips had turned black.

"My name is Ben Gunn," the man said. "I have been living on this island for three years. I eat berries and the meat of wild goats. But at night I dream of cheese—toasted cheese. Do you have any cheese with you?"

"No," I said. "But there is plenty of cheese on my ship. Tell me, how did you get here? Were you shipwrecked?"

"Marooned," he answered.

I knew what that meant. That was how pirates punished members of their crew. They left them behind on a deserted island.

Ben Gunn told me how he got marooned. He had been on Captain Flint's ship when Flint buried his treasure. A few years later he came back to the island in another ship. He told the crew about the treasure. They searched for twelve days. When they found nothing, they thought Ben had lied to them. So they left him on the island and sailed away.

"But now I am rich." Ben Gunn laughed. "Rich." He could not stop giggling. Then he reached out and pinched me—hard!

Ben Gunn wasn't happy to hear that Long John was back on Treasure

Island. He promised to help me and my friends. All he wanted in return was a share of Captain Flint's treasure.

I gave my promise. But I wasn't sure Ben Gunn would be much help. He kept giggling and pinching me. A lot of what he said made no sense. I thought he had been alone so long that he had lost his mind.

Ben Gunn offered to lend me his homemade boat so I could get back to the ship. We were on our way to the boat's hiding place when we heard a loud noise, like thunder. It was a cannon shot!

Up ahead I saw a small fort made out of logs. This fort was marked on our treasure map. But I was surprised to see our ship's flag flying over it.

"Your friends must be inside that fort," Ben Gunn said. "The pirates would never fly the British flag. They would fly the pirates' flag—the Jolly Roger."

I could hardly wait to join my friends. But Ben Gunn refused to come along. He told me that he had a secret cave in the forest. He would feel safer there. As we said good-bye, Ben started giggling again. "If those pirates camp on shore tonight, so much the worse for them," he said.

7. The Fight Begins

Much later Dr. Livesey told me how he and the others came to be inside the fort. When the doctor found out I had gone ashore with Long John, he was worried. He rowed to the beach and found the log fort.

The fort was not very strong. It was just a one-room cabin surrounded by a wall made of logs. But there was a spring inside the wall, and the *Hispaniola* was low on water. So the squire and the captain decided they would be better off at the fort.

The squire gave old Tom Redruth a pistol. Redruth stood guard over the six sailors that Long John had left on the ship. In the meantime the squire and the others made several trips to the fort. They took all the weapons off the ship, and the food, too.

When it came time for the last trip to shore, Redruth came along. So did one of the six sailors, a man named Mr. Gray. "I have had enough of this pirate business," he said. "I will take my chances with you."

While they were rowing to shore, the sailors on the *Hispaniola* got loose. They fired the ship's cannon. That was the shot Ben and I heard. Long John and the others on shore heard the shot too. They came running, and a fight broke out. Poor Tom Redruth got killed. So did one of Long John's men.

The pirates captured the lifeboat and some of our supplies. But except for old Tom Redruth, all my friends made it safely to the fort.

When I got to the fort, the squire and the doctor were very glad to see me. They were surprised that I was still alive. I told them all about Ben Gunn. But it was hard to see what the strange little man could do to stop Long John Silver.

The pirates' camp was so close we could hear them. They sang pirate songs as loud as they could. It sounded as if they were having a wonderful time.

The next morning Long John Silver showed up at the fort. With him was another pirate. They were carrying a white flag, and they wanted to have a talk.

During the night someone had sneaked into the pirate camp and killed a man. Long John thought we had done it. We knew that the real killer must be Ben Gunn. But we didn't tell Long John that.

Now Long John wanted to make a deal. "We want your map," he said. In exchange for the treasure map, he promised to give us half the supplies. The pirates would take the treasure, but they would spare our lives. Once they were safe, they would let the British Navy know where we were. The navy would send a ship to rescue us.

We weren't ready to give up yet. "I

have a deal of my own," said Captain Smollett. "Surrender now and we'll see you get a fair trial."

Long John just laughed at that. He and the other pirate turned and disappeared into the forest.

A few hours later the pirates attacked. Some hid in the trees and shot at us. Four of the bravest of them rushed the fort. They were as quick

as monkeys. In a minute they were over the wall.

"Out, lads! Fight 'em in the open," shouted Captain Smollett. We started to obey. But one pirate was already in the cabin. Waving his sword, he took out after Dr. Livesey.

Bullets flew everywhere. Everyone was shouting. There was so much smoke that I couldn't see who was winning the fight.

When the smoke finally cleared, five pirates were dead. But our Mr. Joyce had been killed too. And Mr. Hunter was badly wounded. A few hours later he died.

Now there were just nine pirates left. But only five of us: Dr. Livesey. Squire Trelawney. Captain Smollett. Mr. Gray, the sailor who had come over to our side. And me.

8. My Sea Adventure

After the battle ended, Dr. Livesey took the treasure map and went off to talk to Ben Gunn.

I had an idea too. I was afraid the pirates would take the *Hispaniola* and leave us marooned. I had a plan to stop them. It was so dangerous that I knew the others would never let me try it. So I waited until no one was watching, and I sneaked out of the fort.

Ben Gunn had told me where his little boat was hidden. It did not take me long to find it. The boat was made of wood, covered with goatskins. It was as round as a teacup. A round boat is hard to row. But I made it out to our ship.

This was my plan: I would cut the *Hispaniola* loose from its anchor. The ship would drift in to shore and get stuck in the sand. Later we could pull it free. But for now the pirates could not sail away and leave us marooned.

There was a rope hanging over the stern of the ship. As soon as I tied up my little boat, I climbed up the rope. Hanging from it, I was able to peer through the cabin window. Israel Hands and another pirate were inside the cabin.

The two of them had been left by Long John to guard the ship. But they had gotten into an argument. They were so busy fighting that they didn't even see me watching them.

I climbed back down the rope and cut the ship's anchor. The *Hispaniola* started drifting. I was right behind her in my little boat. Suddenly a strong wind came up. This was not part of my plan at all. The ship started moving faster and faster. So did my boat. We were caught in a fast current. And we were being swept around to the other side of the island.

Soon the waves were huge. I rowed with all my might. But I could not get back to shore. The big ship and the little boat kept drifting around the island. No one seemed to be sailing the *Hispaniola*. I wondered why Mr. Hands and the other man didn't stop fighting and save the ship.

We drifted all night. By morning we had reached the southwest tip of Treasure Island.

By now I was very thirsty. If I stayed on my little boat I would be swept far out to sea. I would surely die. I was so tired I wanted to give up. But I knew I had to keep my wits about me. My only hope was to get on board the *Hispaniola*.

I began rowing toward the big ship. But just then the wind changed again. The *Hispaniola* began to turn around in circles. She tossed up and down on the waves. Suddenly the ship was headed right for my little boat.

The jib boom—the long pole that held one of the sails—was swinging free. When it swung right over my head, I reached up and grabbed it. I held on tight.

Seconds later I heard a loud crack. The *Hispaniola* had run right over the little boat. It sank quickly out of sight.

I scrambled onto the deck. The first thing I saw was one of the two sailors. He was dead, killed in last night's fight. Israel Hands lay nearby, alive but wounded. His leg seemed to be badly hurt.

"I am taking over the ship," I told him.

Mr. Hands looked up at me. "Very well, Captain Hawkins," he said. "I'll obey you. I have no choice."

I knew there was a small cove on the north side of the island. I decided to hide the *Hispaniola* there. Israel Hands helped me steer the ship. He didn't want to drift out to sea any more than I did. But soon he began to complain. "I'm thirsty," he said.

"Won't you go below and get me something to drink?"

I went. But I did not trust Mr. Hands. Before I went below, I sneaked a look back at him. As soon as he thought I was gone, he started to walk perfectly well. He found a bloody knife lying on the deck. He hid it inside his shirt.

I pretended not to know about the knife. When I came back on deck, Mr. Hands was limping again. Together we hauled at the sails. We got the ship safely into the cove.

For a few minutes I was so busy that I almost forgot that Mr. Hands was just pretending to be badly hurt. But all of a sudden something made me turn around. He had sneaked up behind me! He pulled out the knife. Then he charged.

As quickly as I could, I jumped out of the way. I grabbed the ship's rudder and gave it a hard shove. The rudder hit Mr. Hands in the chest. Then I remembered that I had brought two pistols with me from the fort. I reached into my pocket and pulled out one of them. I took aim and fired.

But nothing happened! The powder in the pistol was wet.

Mr. Hands began chasing me around the deck. I got a lead on him and climbed up the mast. I am a fast climber. Safe in my high perch, I had time to reload both pistols with dry powder.

But now Mr. Hands was coming after me. "Not a step closer," I warned him.

Mr. Hands stopped cold. He had been carrying his knife in his teeth. Now he took it out and spoke. "I guess we'll have to make a truce," he said.

I was feeling proud of myself. I had won the fight. But at that moment Mr. Hands reached back and threw his knife. It sang through the air.

I felt a sharp pain in my shoulder. At the same instant, I heard two shots. My pistols had gone off. I don't even remember firing them.

Mr. Hands gasped and fell backward. He hit the water with a smack.

I would have fallen too, but the knife had pinned my shirt to the mast. I had killed a man! The horror of it made me feel sick inside.

I stared down at the green water. It was so clear that I could see Mr. Hands's body lying on the bottom. Whatever happened, I didn't want to fall into the water beside him. I pulled myself free and climbed back down to the deck.

9. Captain Silver

My shoulder was cut, but the wound was not very bad. I knew I would be all right. And the *Hispaniola* was safely hidden in the cove. My plan had worked after all.

By now it was night again. Quietly, I waded to shore and made my way back across the island to the fort. Without making a sound I climbed over the wall and crawled back into the little log building. I could hear my friends snoring nearby.

Just as I was lying down I hit something with my foot. It was a man's leg. He groaned softly. Then a scream rang out.

"Pieces of eight! Pieces of eight!"

I would have known that voice anywhere. It was Long John Silver's green parrot.

It was too late to run away. The pirates had taken over the fort. Two of them tackled me and held on tight. Now I was their prisoner.

Long John Silver was grinning from ear to ear. "So here's Jim Hawkins," he said. "Dropped in for a visit."

"Where are my friends?" I demanded.

"Gone," said Long John. He explained that the squire and the others had made a truce with him. They had left their supplies to the pirates and gone off into the woods. I was glad to hear that my friends were still alive. But why would they give up the fort? Had they gone mad?

Long John told me I might as well side with the pirates now. The squire and the doctor thought I had run away.

But I could see that things weren't going well for Long John, either.

Another of the pirates had died. Counting Long John, there were only six men left in the fort. Now some of them had come down with fevers.

On top of all their other troubles, the pirates thought that Israel Hands had taken the ship and left them marooned.

Soon the pirates started to talk among themselves. "All this is the boy's fault," one of them said. "He's the one who took Billy Bones's map." To get revenge, the pirates were going to kill me.

I knew I had to talk fast to save my life. "I was the one who found out about your plan to take over the ship," I said bravely. "And I'm the one who took the *Hispaniola*. Kill me if you want. But it won't do any good. And if you let me live, I'll speak up for you after we're rescued. I'll see that you don't hang."

The pirates didn't pay any attention. They were going to kill me anyway. But Long John took my side.

"Kill him and you'll have to kill me, too," he told his crew.

The other pirates thought this might not be a bad idea. They were sick of taking orders from Long John. They went outside to talk it over.

As soon as they were gone, Long John started to bargain with me. "I'll save my life and yours, too," he said. "But you must do the same for me. After we're caught, tell your friends that I stood up for you. Whatever happens, make sure they don't hang me."

I promised to do just that.

Soon the crew returned. One of the men stepped forward. He handed Long John a piece of paper. It was the black spot. They had decided to kill him, and me too.

But Long John didn't seem afraid.

"I'm still the captain here," said he. "You say I made a hash of this cruise. Why, it's you lads who sank our plan!"

Long John reminded the pirates that they were the ones who had been too greedy to wait until the treasure was dug up. He told them that they would never get along without him. Besides, he said, things weren't so bad after all. He told them the *Hispaniola* was hidden safely nearby. "Jim here is our last hope," he added. They could use me as a hostage.

Long John was smart. The pirates weren't used to thinking for themselves. They were starting to change their minds about killing him. Then he reached inside his dirty shirt. He pulled out a piece of paper and threw it down on the floor. "I made a good bargain with the doctor," he told them. "Look what he gave me."

It was the treasure map with the three X's! The pirates were so excited that they forgot all about the black spot.

But my heart sank. Why would the doctor give the map to Long John? Now I was sure my friends had lost their minds.

10. Flint's Treasure

The next morning Dr. Livesey came to the fort. He was carrying a flag of truce. By now several of the pirates were very sick. Even though they were his enemies, Dr. Livesey was still a doctor. He had brought medicine for them.

I needed to talk to the doctor alone. Long John decided to let me. But he made me give my word of honor that I wouldn't try to run away.

"So, Jim, you've joined the pirates

now," said the doctor.

"I have not!" I answered. I explained how the pirates had captured me. I also told him where I had hidden the ship.

"The ship is safe!" Dr. Livesey was delighted. "You've saved us at every turn," he said.

The doctor wanted us to make a run for it right then. But I knew we'd never get away. The pirates would shoot us down. Besides, I had made a promise to Long John. He might be a pirate and a liar, but I was not. I would not go against my word of honor.

Before the doctor left, he gave Long John a warning. "I wouldn't go near that treasure if I were you," he said. "You might run into trouble."

Of course the pirates paid no attention.

I could see that none of them ever thought ahead. The little fort was a mess. When the pirates cooked breakfast, they made more food than they could possibly eat. What they didn't finish, they threw into the fire. At that rate, it wouldn't take them long to use up their supplies.

After breakfast the men were ready to go hunting for treasure. Long John decided to take me with them. He tied a rope around my waist. He held the other end of the rope in his mouth.

"We'll use Jim here as a hostage," he told the others. "Once we have the treasure, he'll get his share."

I knew what my share would be. I believed in keeping my promises, but

Long John did not. Once the men had found the treasure, they wouldn't be angry with him anymore. Then he meant to let them kill me.

Down on the beach, we found the lifeboats that the pirates had taken over. We got in one of them and rowed to the spot marked on the map. Then we climbed the flat-topped hill called the Spy-glass. That's where the treasure was supposed to be buried.

The map said to look for a tall tree. But there were lots of tall trees. Which was the right one?

While we were looking around, one of the pirates gave a shout. At the foot of one very tall tree was a skeleton. The skeleton was laid out in a straight line, so that the arm bones seemed to be pointing at something. Long John checked the direction with his compass. The arms pointed east southeast by east.

"By thunder!" said Long John. "We have found Captain Flint's pointer. This was one of the sailors who helped him bury the treasure."

Flint was so evil that just thinking about him made the pirates nervous.

"It's lucky Flint is dead," Long John added. "If he knew we had come for his treasure, this would be a hot spot for us."

"Aye, he's dead," agreed one of the pirates. "But he died bad. If ever a spirit walked, it would be Flint!"

The pirates started to pace off the distance marked on the map. Then, all of a sudden, we heard a faint singing coming from behind one of the tall trees.

"Fifteen men on the dead man's chest.
Yo-ho-ho, and a bottle of rum!"

The pirates stopped in their tracks. "It's Flint!" one of them cried. "It's Flint's ghost!"

"Come, lads," said Long John. "Someone is playing a trick on us."

But the voice started up again, thin

and high. "Darby, Darby McGraw," it sang out. "Fetch the rum."

"That fixes it!" gasped another of the pirates. "Those were Flint's last words. No one could know that but his crew. And we six are the only ones left alive."

"I never heard a ghost with an echo," said Long John. "Besides, I *know* that voice. It's Ben Gunn."

The pirates had thought Ben Gunn was dead too. Still, they cheered up. "I never was afraid of Ben Gunn alive," said one. "I'm not afraid of him dead."

So they kept on pacing off the distance to the treasure. But when they came to the spot marked by the red X on the map, they started to groan and shout. All that was left was a big hole in the ground. There was no gold. Someone had dug it up already.

The pirates were furious. They were ready to shoot me and Long John right there. Quickly, Long John passed me one of his pistols. This time I was sure my life was over. The odds were five against two.

Crack! Crack! Crack! Three shots rang out.

I looked at Long John. He was still standing, and so was I. Neither of us had fired a shot. But two of the pirates had fallen into the empty hole. The other three turned and ran away as fast as they could.

Just then Ben Gunn came running out of the woods. With him were the doctor, the squire, and Mr. Gray. I knew then that I was safe at last.

11. The End of My Story

As soon as everyone caught his breath, Dr. Livesey told me how he had set a trap for the pirates.

While I was away from the fort, the doctor had gone to see Ben Gunn. He learned that Ben had dug up Flint's treasure long ago. That gave the doctor an idea. He told Long John that our side was ready to make a deal. In exchange for some food, we would give up the fort and the map.

Dr. Livesey knew that when the pirates found the empty hole, they would lose their tempers. They would start to fight. With luck, they would kill each other off.

But that was before the doctor knew I was a hostage. When he found out that Long John had me with him, he knew he had to hurry and get help. In the meantime Ben Gunn ran up Spy-glass Hill. He kept the pirates busy by pretending to be Flint's ghost.

Now I knew that Ben Gunn wasn't crazy after all. He had saved my life. What's more, he had been telling the truth when he told me he was rich. When we got to his cave in the side of the hill, there was Flint's treasure. I had never seen so much gold. There were gold bars. And pieces of eight. And other kinds of gold pieces, too. Round coins. Square coins. Coins with pictures of all the kings in the world.

Captain Smollett was in the cave too. He had been wounded in the battle for the fort. But he was already feeling better. He was going to be all right.

Later that day we found the *Hispaniola*. For all it had been through, the ship was not in bad shape.

The next morning we started loading Flint's treasure on the ship. There was so much gold that it took us many trips to move it all.

Long John was our prisoner now. The three pirates who ran away were still free, hiding in the forest. But they did not try to stop us. They had had their fill of fighting.

Three days went by. At last the gold was all on board. We set sail for home. We left the three pirates on the island. It was too dangerous to try to take them with us. Later we could send a navy ship to pick them up.

The adventure was over. But not for Long John Silver. Now that he was caught, he tried to change sides again. He reminded Dr. Livesey that he had kept the other pirates from killing me. He claimed that he had been trying to help us all along. "I'm with you hand and glove," he said.

I'll say this for Long John—he never gave up. He could outtalk the devil himself. But this time I knew better than to believe him. I couldn't forget that he had been ready to kill me as soon as he got his hands on the gold.

We had decided to take Long John home to England to stand trial. But we had to make one stop first. We found an island where there was a small village. We left Ben Gunn on the ship to guard our prisoner. The rest of us went ashore to buy food and supplies.

When we got back to the ship, Long John was gone. And so was one small sack of gold from our treasure. Ben Gunn had helped Long John escape. We were amazed. But Ben explained that he was so afraid of Long John that he didn't want to have him on the ship with us. "We're well rid of him," he said.

The journey back to England went quickly. We were sad that poor Mr. Hunter, Mr. Joyce, and Tom Redruth had been killed. Those of us who did make it home were rich, though.

Ben Gunn spent his share of the treasure in a few weeks. Soon he was his old self again, poor but happy. The rest of us were set for life.

As for Long John Silver, we never heard what became of him and his green parrot. But somehow I don't think he came to a good end.

Now that my story is done, I will tell you a secret. There were three X's on Captain Flint's map. One marked the spot where the gold was buried.

That was the treasure we found. Another marked the place where Flint had hidden his guns. The third X showed where he had buried many bars of silver.

As far as I know, the silver is still on Treasure Island. But I'm sure I will never go back to look for it. I would not return to that place for anything in the world.

Lisa Norby has written several other books, including an easy-to-read version of *Kon-Tiki*. When not writing, she loves to travel. She has spent time on exotic islands in many parts of the world, but has yet to find any buried treasure! She lives in Brooklyn, New York.